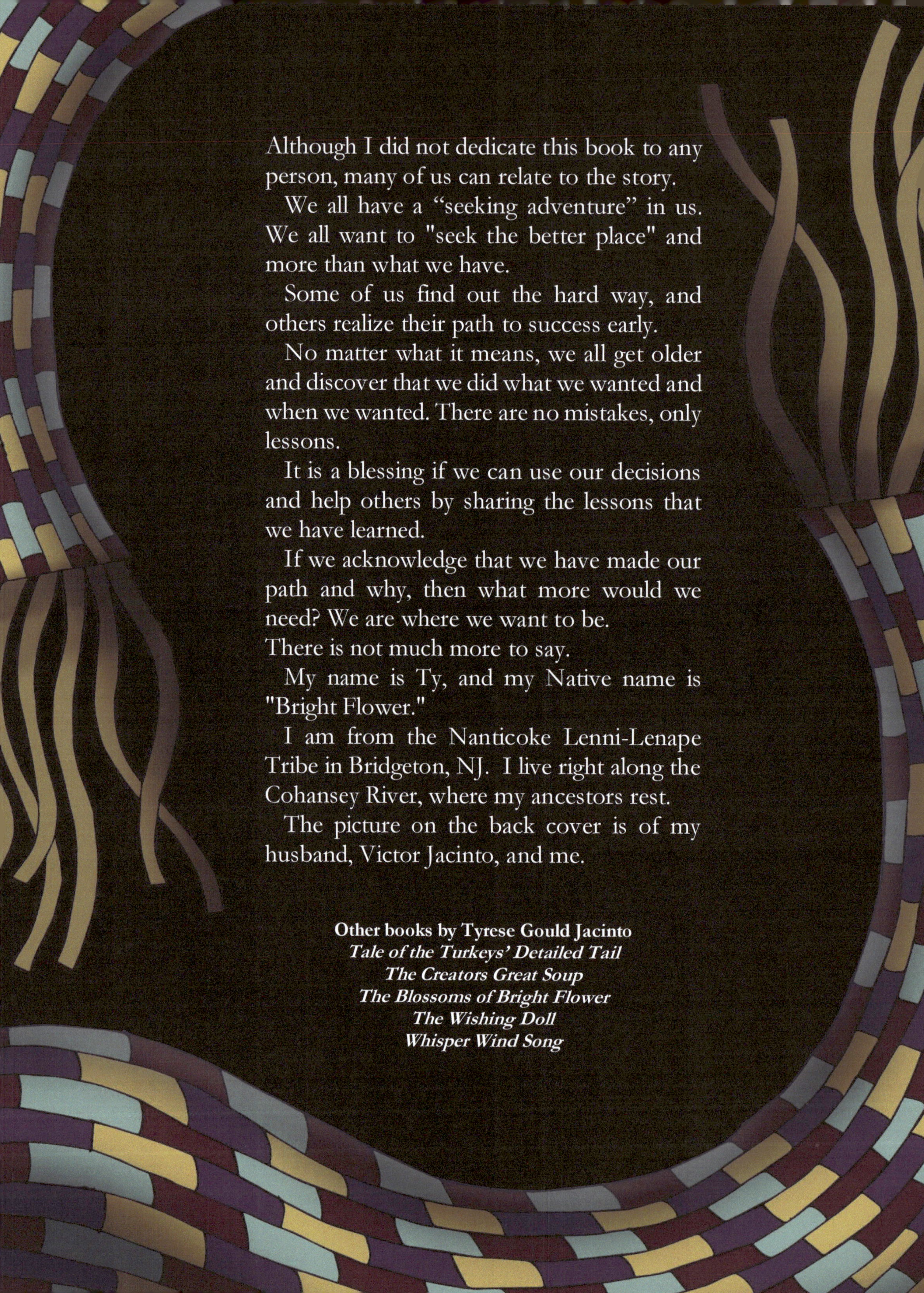

Although I did not dedicate this book to any person, many of us can relate to the story.

We all have a "seeking adventure" in us. We all want to "seek the better place" and more than what we have.

Some of us find out the hard way, and others realize their path to success early.

No matter what it means, we all get older and discover that we did what we wanted and when we wanted. There are no mistakes, only lessons.

It is a blessing if we can use our decisions and help others by sharing the lessons that we have learned.

If we acknowledge that we have made our path and why, then what more would we need? We are where we want to be. There is not much more to say.

My name is Ty, and my Native name is "Bright Flower."

I am from the Nanticoke Lenni-Lenape Tribe in Bridgeton, NJ. I live right along the Cohansey River, where my ancestors rest.

The picture on the back cover is of my husband, Victor Jacinto, and me.

Other books by Tyrese Gould Jacinto
Tale of the Turkeys' Detailed Tail
The Creators Great Soup
The Blossoms of Bright Flower
The Wishing Doll
Whisper Wind Song

This book belongs to:

For my husband Victor and children, George, Annalyse, Adam, Sean, Marcus, Alex, Victor II, Brian, and Jordyn, and my grandchildren, Anastaysia, Nataliya, Caius, Atlas, and Jenavieve

LENAPE PRONUNCIATION GUIDE

www.talk-lenape.org

Tyrese	Ty-ESE
Teksuma	Tek-SUE-ma
Chewanack	Chew-AH-nack
Lenape	Le-NAA-pey
Koamene	Koe-A-men-EE
Mëxumsa	Mahj-HUM-sa

Imprint: Independently published

ISBN: 978-1-969075-06-3

www.TyGouldJacinto.com

Seek the Better Place

A Cohanzick Lenape Tale

Tyrese Gould Jacinto

Illustrated by Arnild C. Aldepolla

Lenape Elders tell a story of a boy named Koamene.

The story goes like this.........

Koamene was from the Cohanzick Lenape village situated right along the bay.

There were many, many villages throughout this vast area. Some villages were separated by long distances that took more than a day to walk, while others were only minutes away.

Koamene's village was large. There were several hundred homes with lots of space between them, surrounded by woods, right between the river inlets and the bay.

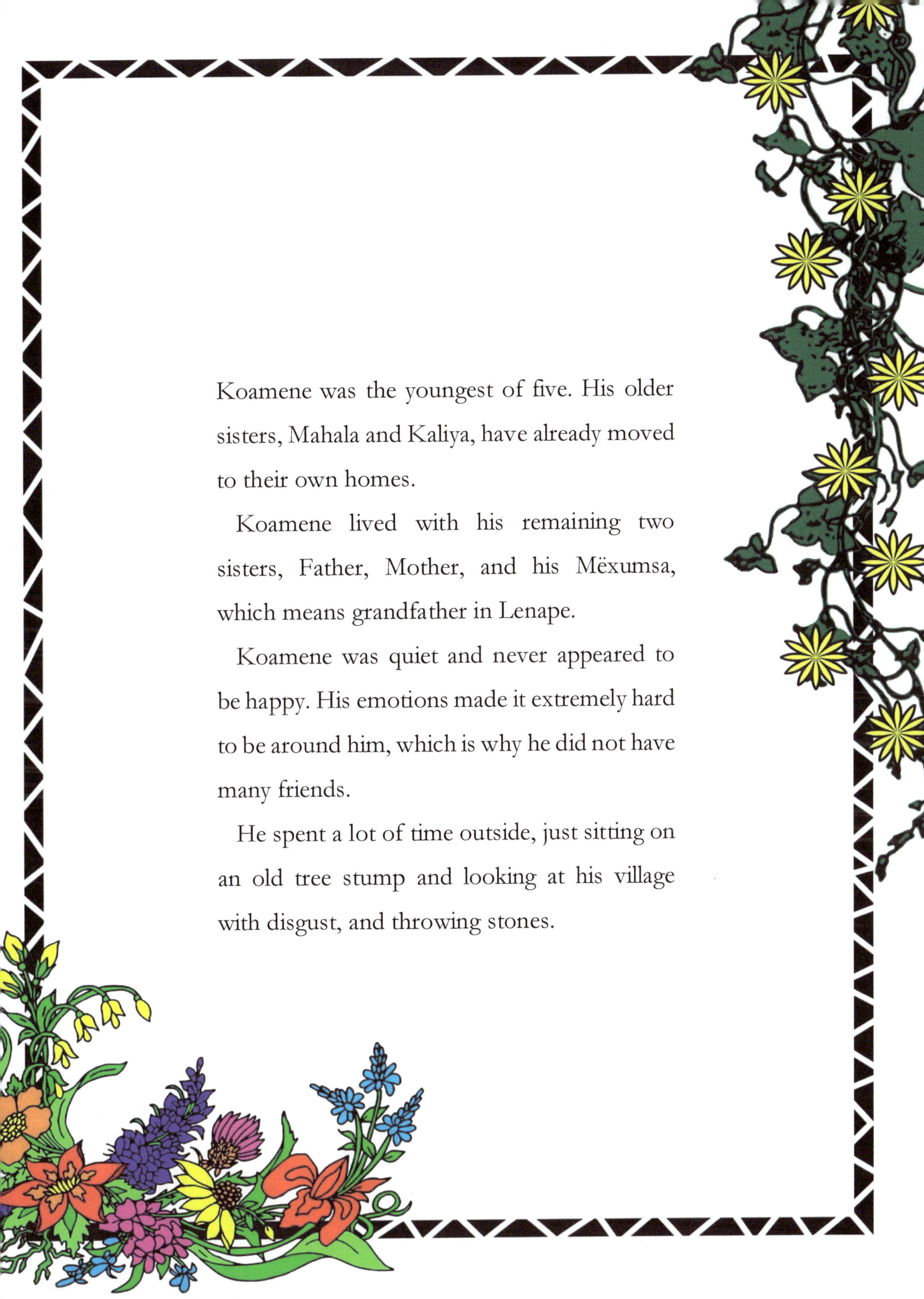

Koamene was the youngest of five. His older sisters, Mahala and Kaliya, have already moved to their own homes.

Koamene lived with his remaining two sisters, Father, Mother, and his Mëxumsa, which means grandfather in Lenape.

Koamene was quiet and never appeared to be happy. His emotions made it extremely hard to be around him, which is why he did not have many friends.

He spent a lot of time outside, just sitting on an old tree stump and looking at his village with disgust, and throwing stones.

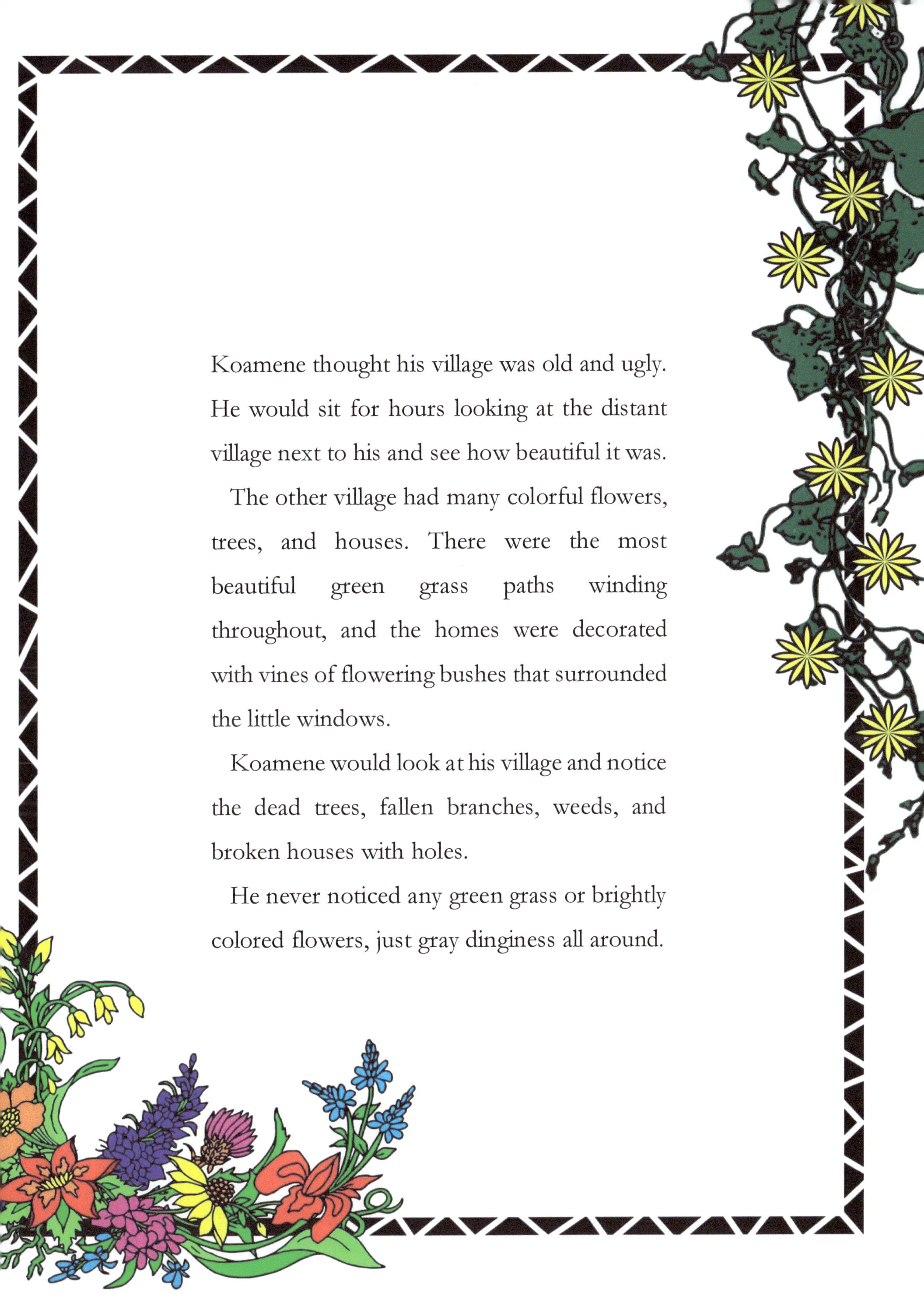

Koamene thought his village was old and ugly. He would sit for hours looking at the distant village next to his and see how beautiful it was.

The other village had many colorful flowers, trees, and houses. There were the most beautiful green grass paths winding throughout, and the homes were decorated with vines of flowering bushes that surrounded the little windows.

Koamene would look at his village and notice the dead trees, fallen branches, weeds, and broken houses with holes.

He never noticed any green grass or brightly colored flowers, just gray dinginess all around.

Occasionally, Koamene would visit one of his friends, Teksuma, who lived in that beautiful village that Koamene so admired.

Teksuma was rich, according to Koamene. His house was beautifully adorned with vining flowers that covered the windows.

Teksuma had clay dishes that were perfect with elaborate designs and oh so colorful. His clothes were of the most beautiful colors, with ideal fringe and beads.

Teksuma had everything that Koamene ever wanted. Koamene was so sad while he visited Teksuma. Koamene did not have the same kind of life, and he could not understand why.

Teksuma was so happy and content that he was always pleasant.

After visiting Teksuma, Koamene always came home sad and depressed.

He just lay in his room under his bear blanket that had bald spots in some places.

He stared out of the ugly hole for a window that was next to his bed.

When he finally decided to arise, which was in the middle of the afternoon, he sat in his house and stared at his Mother's dishes.

He noticed that they have cracks and scratches all around them.

He saw the cup that was on the table, and it had a little chip on the top, and Koamene just thought it was so ugly.

The handmade baskets and hunting tools hanging on the walls were old and dull.

As he went to get up, the chair that he was sitting in shook as if one of the legs was shorter than the rest.

Koamene just said to himself, the chair should be thrown out and never used again.

Koamene kicked the bear rug as he walked through his house because it was dull and had some bald areas. Koamene just thought that the rug was ugly and useless.

He was just so unhappy that he didn't have the things his friend Teksuma had.

He could not understand why.

Koamene was one of the dancers for the tribe. He had regalia that both his Mother and Father made.

He had a long fringe on his shirt, and his leggings fringed at the bottom. His wampum belt was fully beaded.

The belt took his mother six months to make with handmade wampum, which are little shell beads.

Koamene noticed that his belt was missing a few beads, so he just tossed it outside, and it landed next to the stump where he always sat.

He did not consider his Mother's love and the time that she dedicated to making this for him.

Some of the rabbits were nearby and noticed the beaded belt sitting on the ground next to the stump.

One of the rabbits quickly took Koamene's belt into his deep den just under the tree roots and hung it on his little rabbit wall.

All the rabbits in that den were amazed at how beautiful that piece of art was. It was colorful with elaborate flowers made from handmade wampum shells and long hand-twisted leather fringe.

The belt made such a lovely wall hanging for the nice rabbit hole.

Koamene did not notice that Mëxumsa was always watching him, but he was.

Mëxumsa would shake his head in amazement at the display of attitude that Koamene would have.

He was waiting for that moment when he could teach Koamene something new, but Koamene was such a know-it-all, there never seemed to be the right opportunity.

Mëxumsa will wait!

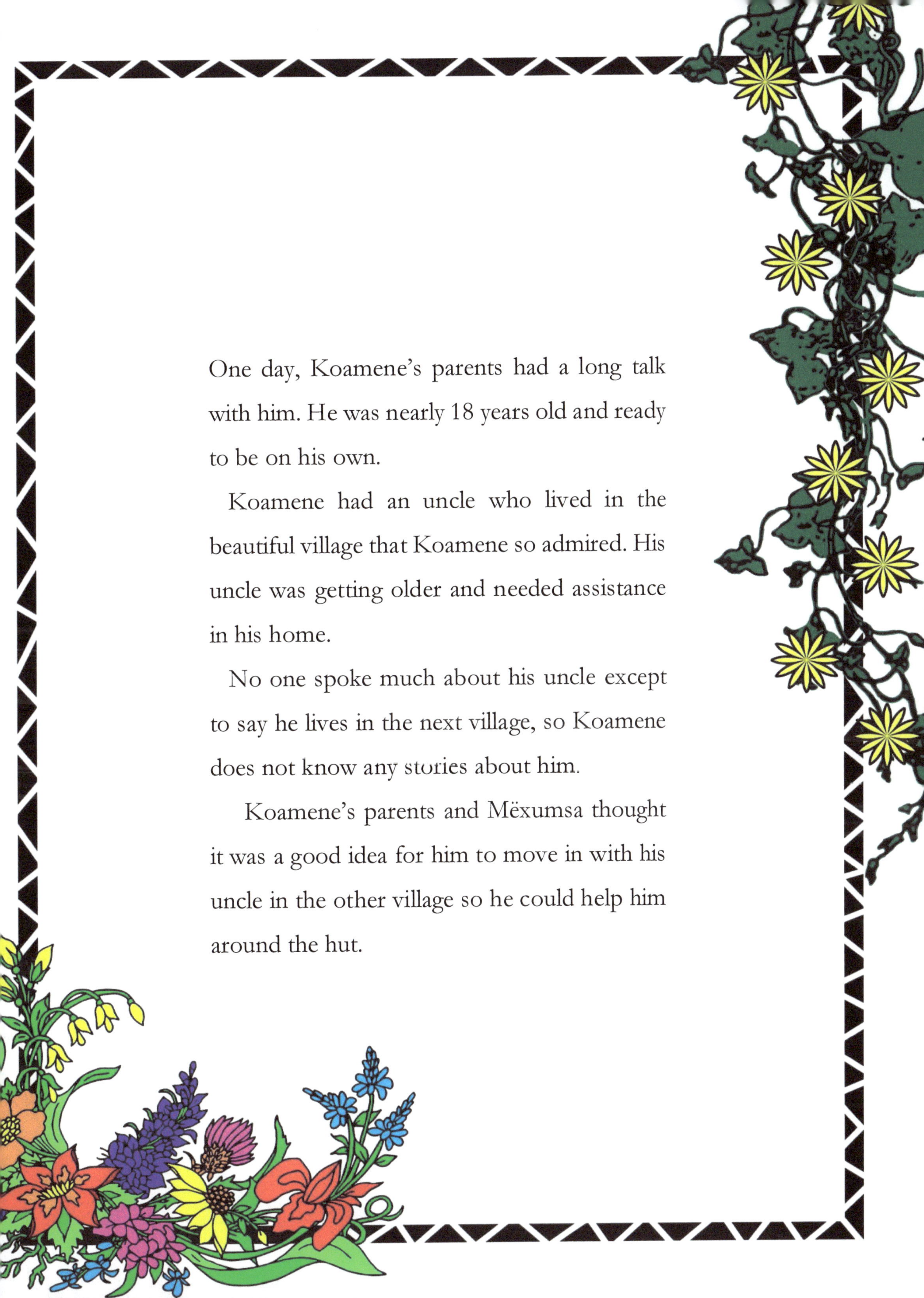

One day, Koamene's parents had a long talk with him. He was nearly 18 years old and ready to be on his own.

Koamene had an uncle who lived in the beautiful village that Koamene so admired. His uncle was getting older and needed assistance in his home.

No one spoke much about his uncle except to say he lives in the next village, so Koamene does not know any stories about him.

Koamene's parents and Mëxumsa thought it was a good idea for him to move in with his uncle in the other village so he could help him around the hut.

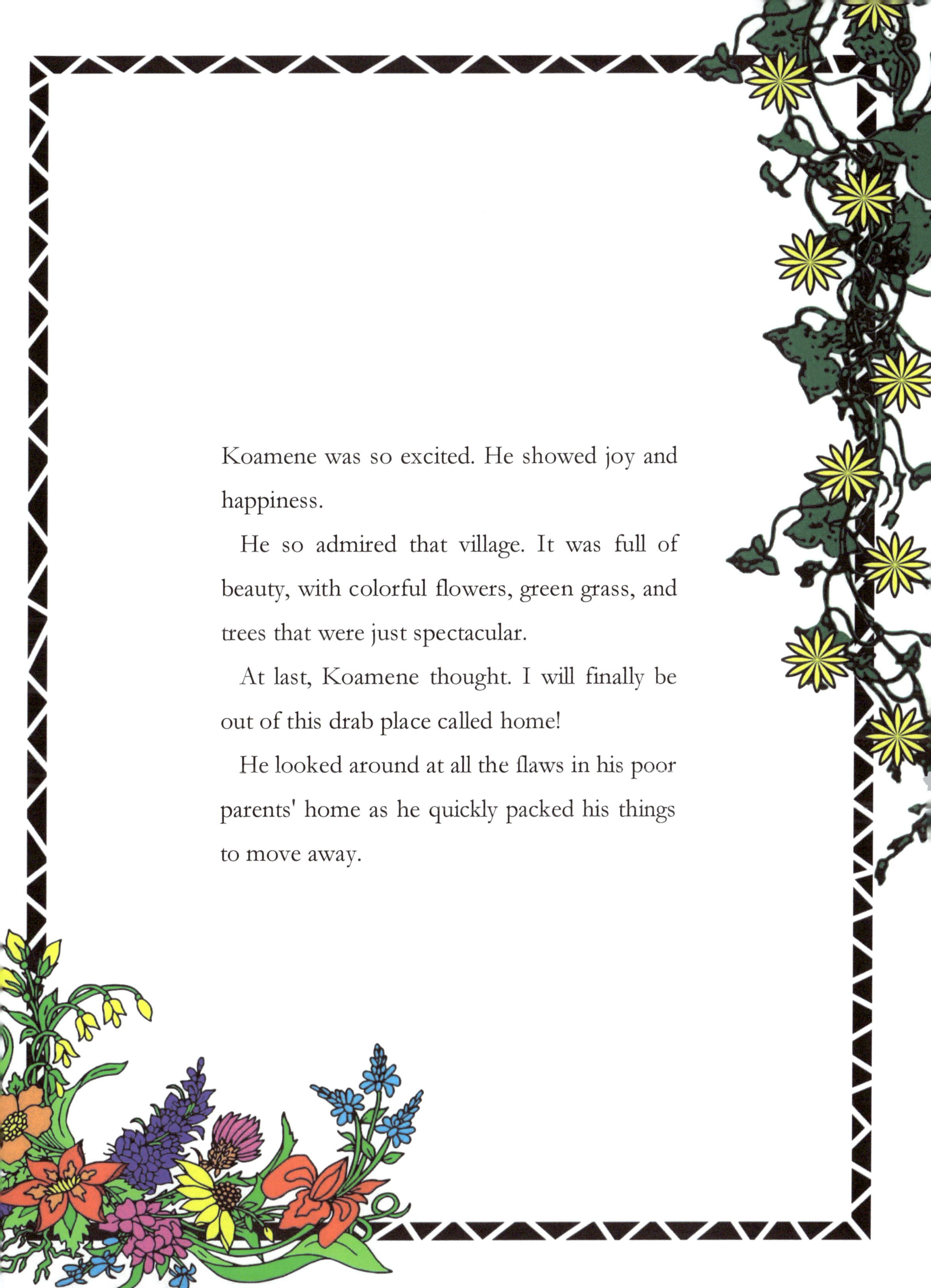

Koamene was so excited. He showed joy and happiness.

He so admired that village. It was full of beauty, with colorful flowers, green grass, and trees that were just spectacular.

At last, Koamene thought. I will finally be out of this drab place called home!

He looked around at all the flaws in his poor parents' home as he quickly packed his things to move away.

Koamene's uncle Chewanack was a legend in his village. They called him "Chew," and he moved to that village 30 years ago from the place where Koamene resides now.

Chew had quite a reputation, and the villagers thought Chew was the coolest.

He never married, always dressed finely, and his house was one of the most beautiful in that village.

Now that Chew was getting older, he was unable to take care of the things around the house.

Chew asked his brother, Koamene's father, if Koamene could stay with him.

Koamene arrived at his uncle Chew's house. He was full of joy as he settled in his new room.

The hut was spectacular, with so many fresh items to view. There were fluffy bear rugs on the floors, and all the shelves on the wall were full of cups and plates with beautifully colorful, flowered designs.

Hanging on the walls were baskets, spears, hatches, bows, and arrows for hunting.

Flowers vines wrapped around his windows, and the grass and trees were a gorgeous dark green.

What a great experience, thought Koamene.

Koamene was glad to help with the chores of the hut. He felt excited to be in the best city that he had ever set eyes on.

He pulled the weeds from around the flowering vines that surrounded the windows. He planted the vegetable garden.

Koamene just enjoyed the daily routine and staying with his uncle. He was finally happy and enjoyed his new life.

Koamene's dream came true.

There was something different about living with Uncle Chew. Koamene noticed that his uncle was quiet and did not have much to say.

Koamene attempted many times to carry on a conversation; however, Chew would not try to speak.

Koamene just took it in stride. He did not give it much thought, nor did he care because he was right where he wanted to be.

He was in the village that he admired much, and this made him happy.

Koamene went to visit his friend Teksuma. He only lived down the lane, a short walk away.

Teksuma noticed that his friend Koamene was different. Koamene was upbeat and happy. He glowed for the first time.

Teksuma enjoyed the new attitude. He always worried about his good friend Koamene. He liked him just the same.

They had a great visit together, throwing some rocks in the river, catching fish, walking around the village, and admiring the beauty.

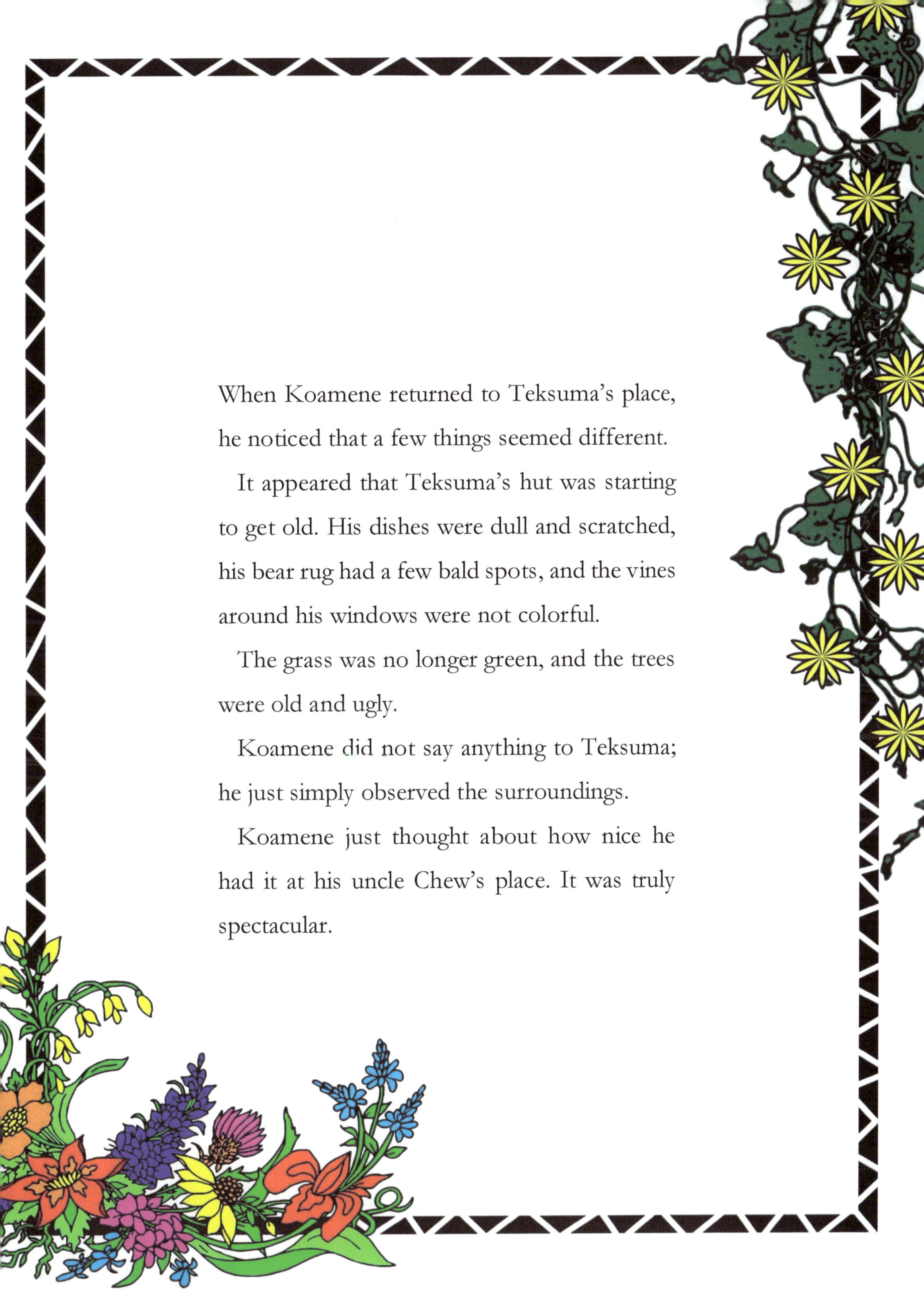

When Koamene returned to Teksuma's place, he noticed that a few things seemed different.

It appeared that Teksuma's hut was starting to get old. His dishes were dull and scratched, his bear rug had a few bald spots, and the vines around his windows were not colorful.

The grass was no longer green, and the trees were old and ugly.

Koamene did not say anything to Teksuma; he just simply observed the surroundings.

Koamene just thought about how nice he had it at his uncle Chew's place. It was truly spectacular.

Koamene arrived home at his uncle Chews.

As soon as he entered the hut, his Uncle Chew confronted him with a loud, angry voice.

"You are old enough to take care of your responsibilities without me telling you what to do!" said his uncle Chew.

Koamene, taken by surprise, never heard his uncle say much, let alone yell. It was a total surprise.

Is this something to look forward to as usual? Is this what it was going to be like from now on? He thought to himself, Am I going to have to work?

His world was changing, and ever so fast! Uncle Chew then left to visit the town.

Koamene quickly began to work. He started pulling weeds, tilling the garden, sweeping the walk areas, patching the little holes in the hut, and gathering more reeds to fill in any spaces.

Koamene cleaned the entire area around the hut. He cleaned piles of leaves that had gathered around the vining flowers that surrounded the windows.

Koamene removed all the broken branches that littered the area and even chopped down a dead tree that was near his window.

Koamene was content and satisfied with his accomplishments, and he would seek his Uncle Chew's approval.

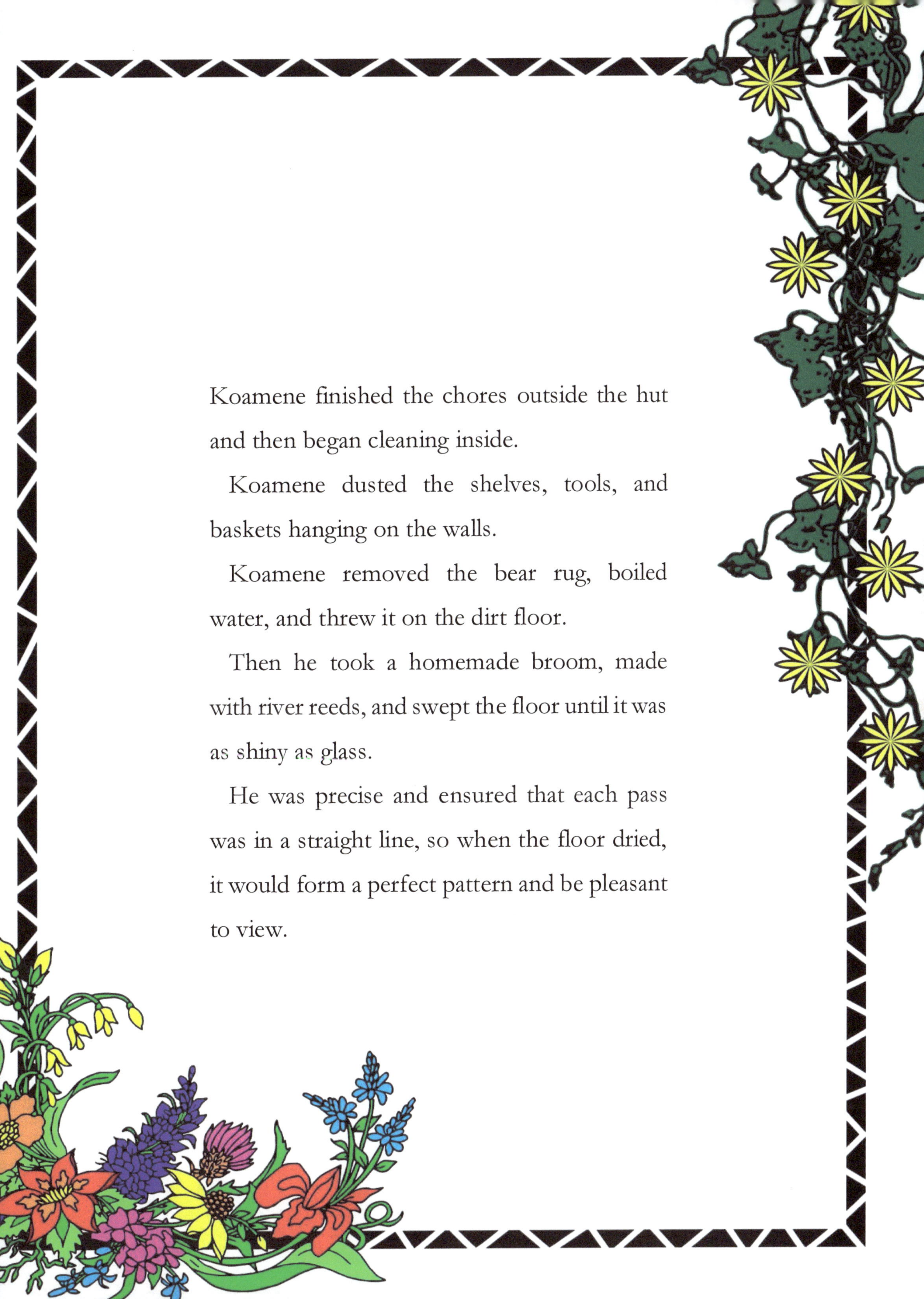

Koamene finished the chores outside the hut and then began cleaning inside.

Koamene dusted the shelves, tools, and baskets hanging on the walls.

Koamene removed the bear rug, boiled water, and threw it on the dirt floor.

Then he took a homemade broom, made with river reeds, and swept the floor until it was as shiny as glass.

He was precise and ensured that each pass was in a straight line, so when the floor dried, it would form a perfect pattern and be pleasant to view.

While the floor was drying out, he took the deerskins and bearskin blankets outside and hung them on a tree branch to beat the dust out of them with a large stick.

And lastly, he did the same with the bearskin rugs that he removed earlier.

He beat each one until there was no presence of dust while they swayed in the wind.

There were many blankets and rugs, and this took some time and a lot of muscle to finish.

Koamene took all the clay dishes outside and washed them in the river one by one, being ever so careful not to damage the intricate patterns and designs of the handmade pottery dishes.

He noticed that the dishes were a little scratched with a few cracks. He never saw that before. He also noticed that some of the paint was dull and faded. He wondered to himself if he was the cause of this.

Koamene hoped that he did not cause damage to his uncle's beautiful pottery.

When Koamene completed washing the dishes, he washed his Uncle Chew's clothes as well as his own clothes in the river alongside his hut.

While washing his uncle's clothes, he noticed that the leather was fragile and had many little holes from being worn for so long.

They always appeared beautiful and new. Koamene's uncle was still an elegant dresser, and Koamene never noticed these flaws before.

Koamene was concerned that he had caused damage to his uncle's clothes.

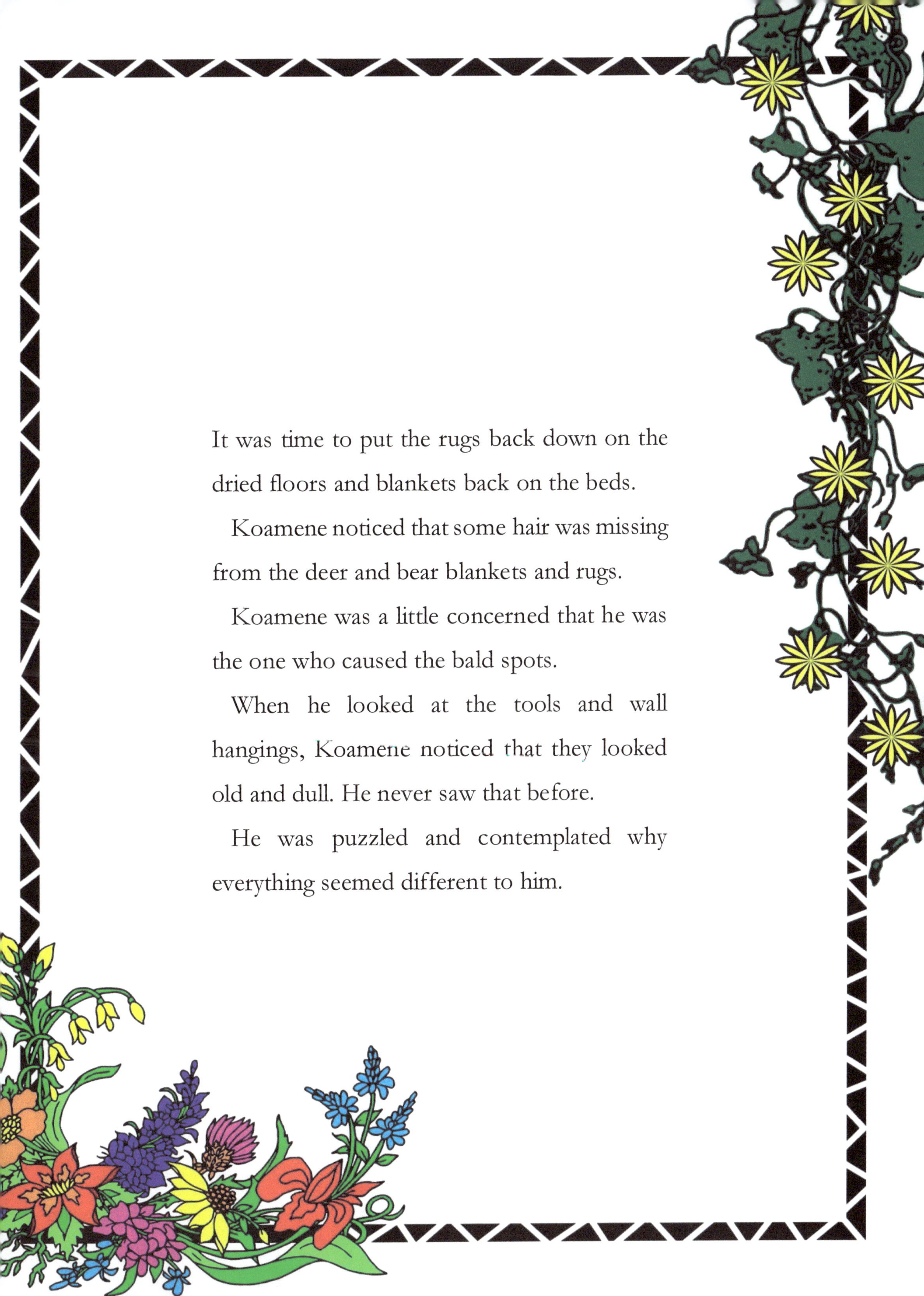

It was time to put the rugs back down on the dried floors and blankets back on the beds.

Koamene noticed that some hair was missing from the deer and bear blankets and rugs.

Koamene was a little concerned that he was the one who caused the bald spots.

When he looked at the tools and wall hangings, Koamene noticed that they looked old and dull. He never saw that before.

He was puzzled and contemplated why everything seemed different to him.

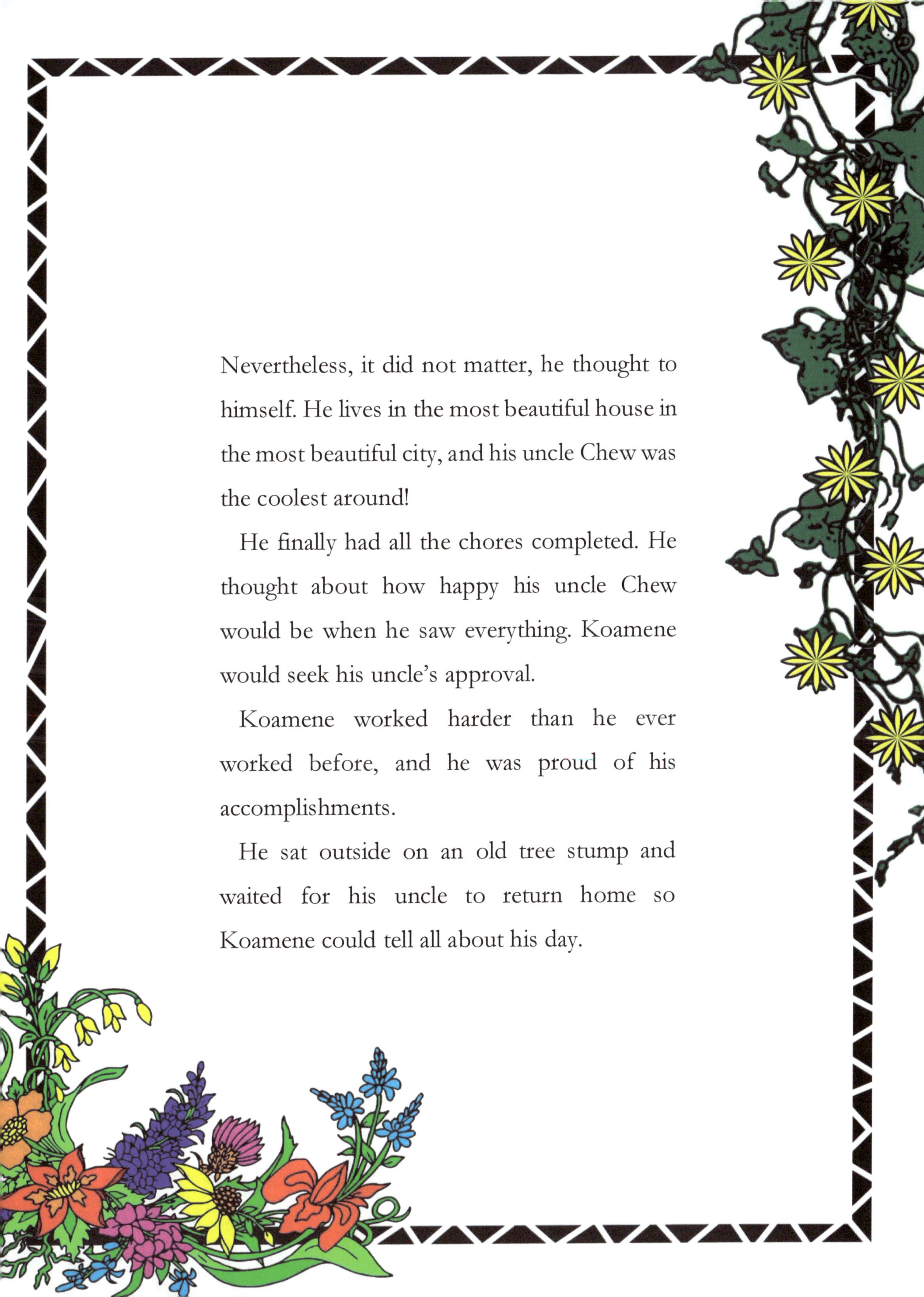

Nevertheless, it did not matter, he thought to himself. He lives in the most beautiful house in the most beautiful city, and his uncle Chew was the coolest around!

He finally had all the chores completed. He thought about how happy his uncle Chew would be when he saw everything. Koamene would seek his uncle's approval.

Koamene worked harder than he ever worked before, and he was proud of his accomplishments.

He sat outside on an old tree stump and waited for his uncle to return home so Koamene could tell all about his day.

Uncle Chew finally arrived home, and Koamene was beaming with excitement.

He stood up from the stump and waited to greet Uncle Chew as he walked up to the hut.

Uncle Chew breezed right by Koamene, groaned a muddled noise, and did not acknowledge Koamene as he quickly ran into the hut.

Koamene felt crushed. Uncle Chew not only did not see him, but he also did not notice all the work he accomplished around the hut.

He pulled weeds, tilled the garden, and even cut down an old tree.

How could his Uncle be such an inconsiderate, thought Koamene?

Koamene followed Uncle Chew into the hut to try to get his uncle's attention.

Uncle Chew ran right by all the work that Koamene did and never acknowledged any of the work.

Koamene was devastated. He did not know how to take the attitude that his uncle was displaying. He sought his uncle's approval.

He worked so hard, dusted the shelves, tools, and baskets, glazed the floors, beat the rugs and blankets, and his uncle did not acknowledge anything.

How could he be so mean and treat his nephew this way?

Koamene ran outside and plopped down on the tree stump outside the door.

He was sobbing quietly and felt lonely and depressed. He wondered if this was the way it was going to be. How could he live like this?

As Koamene sat sobbing, he noticed that the grass was not so green; it was a dull yellow.

He noticed that the vining flowers looked like weeds that surrounded the windows. There were dead trees everywhere.

He thought to himself that this place was not better than his old village.

It was dull and not so lovely as he had always thought it was before he moved there.

He sat with disgust at the way everything looked in his once beautiful new village.

It was time for bed, and Koamene went inside.

He noticed his uncle sitting at the table, drinking a cup of water. Koamene noticed that the cup had a large scratch and was dull.

The table was old and brittle. Koamene never noticed this before. Each time his uncle took a sip, the table shook, as if there was one shorter leg.

The hut was dull and gray. Koamene did not notice before, but it was not as beautiful as he had previously perceived it to be.

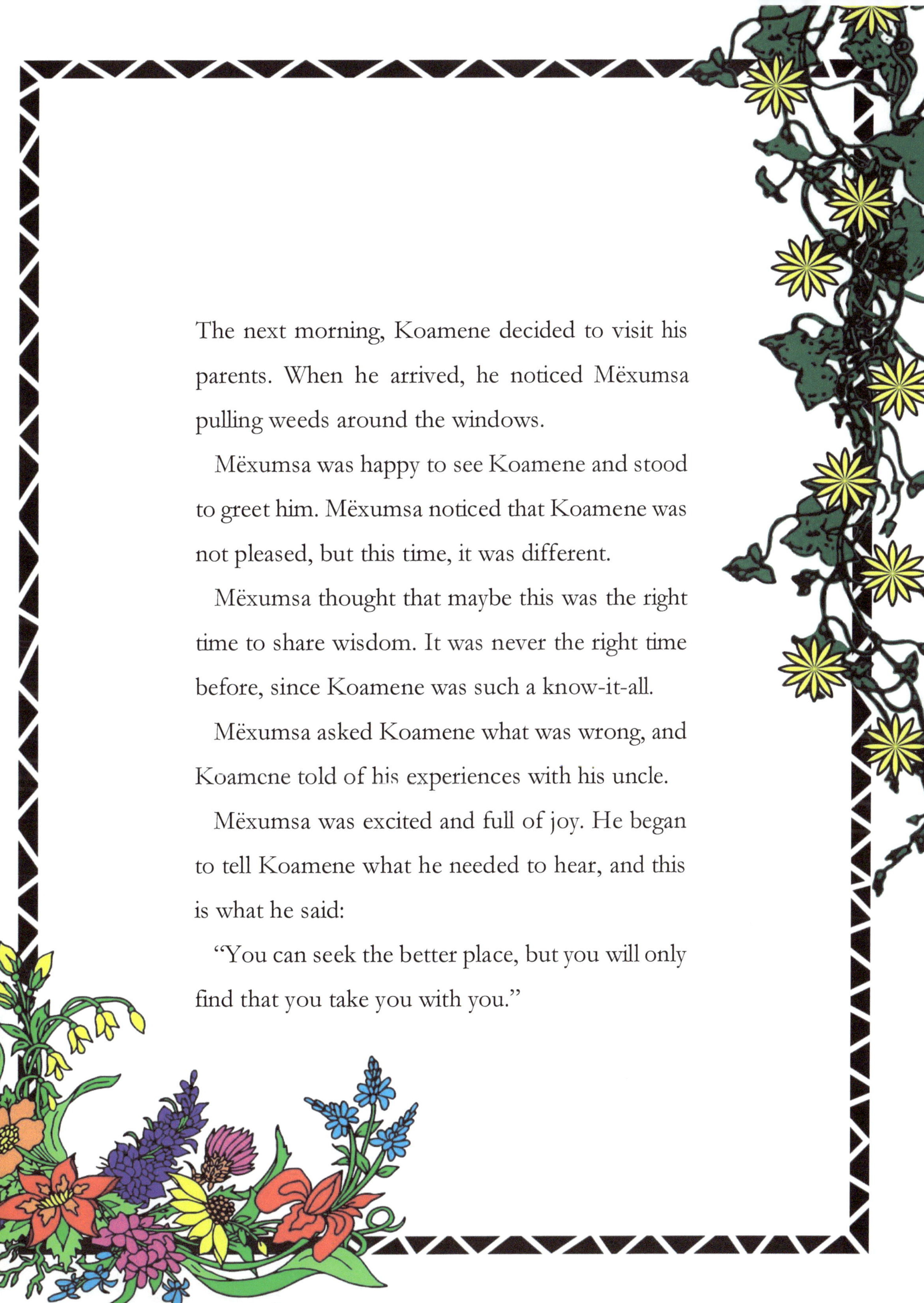

The next morning, Koamene decided to visit his parents. When he arrived, he noticed Mëxumsa pulling weeds around the windows.

Mëxumsa was happy to see Koamene and stood to greet him. Mëxumsa noticed that Koamene was not pleased, but this time, it was different.

Mëxumsa thought that maybe this was the right time to share wisdom. It was never the right time before, since Koamene was such a know-it-all.

Mëxumsa asked Koamene what was wrong, and Koamene told of his experiences with his uncle.

Mëxumsa was excited and full of joy. He began to tell Koamene what he needed to hear, and this is what he said:

"You can seek the better place, but you will only find that you take you with you."

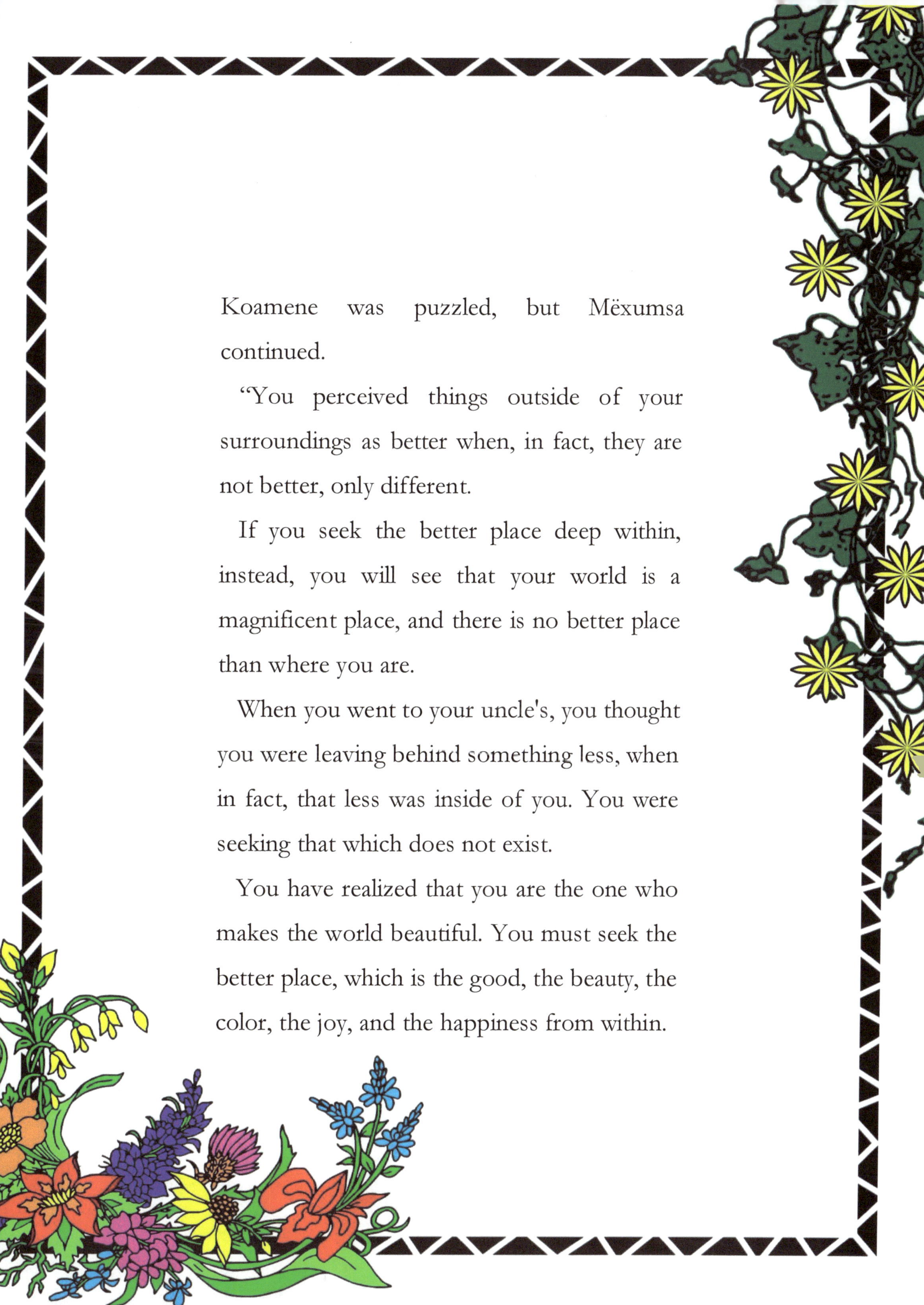

Koamene was puzzled, but Mëxumsa continued.

"You perceived things outside of your surroundings as better when, in fact, they are not better, only different.

If you seek the better place deep within, instead, you will see that your world is a magnificent place, and there is no better place than where you are.

When you went to your uncle's, you thought you were leaving behind something less, when in fact, that less was inside of you. You were seeking that which does not exist.

You have realized that you are the one who makes the world beautiful. You must seek the better place, which is the good, the beauty, the color, the joy, and the happiness from within.

These things come from within you, and you cannot find them by seeking on the outside."

From that very moment, Koamene's world was different. He noticed that everything around him was colorful. He saw the little flowers, the bright vines that surrounded his mom's windows.

He noticed that the dishes had intricate designs and colors.

As he sat on his old tree stump, he noticed a long string of leather coming from under the tree roots.

As he pulled the string of leather, out popped his wampum belt. It was so beautiful. Many different colored wampum shells made a beautiful pattern.

Koamene was happy. This time, it was a genuine feeling of joy. His world healed. His seeking and perspective healed.

Koamene would never be sad again, and he enjoyed his village and meditated on his Mëxumsa's lesson from that moment.

He only seeks the better place from within himself.

He realizes that wherever he goes, he takes himself.

Bright
Oy
Flower